Fenton's Leap

by Libba Moore Gray

illustrated by
Jo-Ellen Bosson

Simon & Schuster Books for Young Readers
Published by Simon & Schuster
New York • London • Toronto • Sydney • Tokyo • Singapore

SIMON & SCHUSTER BOOKS FOR YOUNG READERS
Simon & Schuster Building, Rockefeller Center,
1230 Avenue of the Americas, New York, New York 10020.
Text copyright © 1994 by Libba Moore Gray.
Illustrations copyright © 1994 by Jo-Ellen Bosson.
All rights reserved including the right of reproduction in whole or
in part in any form. SIMON & SCHUSTER BOOKS FOR YOUNG READERS is a
trademark of Simon & Schuster.

Designed by David Neuhaus.
The text of this book is set in 16 point Usherwood Medium. The illustrations
were done in watercolor. Manufactured in the United States of America.

10 9 8 7 6 5 4 3 2 1

Library of Congress Cataloging-in-Publication Data
Gray, Libba Moore. Fenton's leap / by Libba Moore Gray ;
illustrated by Jo-Ellen Bosson.   p.   cm.
Summary: Fenton the near-sighted frog stumbles from one
danger to another, until a pair of eyeglasses opens up
a new world of clear vision to him.
[1. Eyeglasses—Fiction.   2. Frogs—Fiction.   3. Animals—Fiction.]
I. Bosson, Jo-Ellen, ill. II. Title. PZ7.G7793Fe   1993
[E]—dc20   92-19648   CIP

ISBN: 0-671-79196-6

For my sister, Suzanne, and my brother, Michael, and
for my children, Michael, Amy, David, and especially
Rachel, who gave me the idea for the story —L.M.G.

For E.R.B. —J-E. B.

Down in a green deep bog where lily pads floated like flat little boats and polliwogs swam in wiggles and wags and the smell of jasmine filled the air, lived a very nearsighted frog named Fenton.

When his cousins went
Splish, Splash, Splosh,
Fenton went *SPLAT!*

When they jumped with a *Bound, Bounce, Boing,*
Fenton went *BLAT!*

And so it went for Fenton, day after day, jump after jump,
hop after hop, leap after leap.

One day in the middle of a very merry game of Leap Frog, the cousins went *Splish, Splash, Splosh*.

Fenton went *SPLAT* right in the center of a moss-covered log where a scruffy-winged, very hungry owl waited for lunch.

"Jump, Fenton! Hop, Fenton! Leap, Fenton!" croaked the cousins.

nd he looped and he dropped with a plop just
the owl's sharp yellow claws and right onto the
long ripple-backed alligator.

Gurgle glub went the green-black water into the
outh.

ton! Hop, Fenton! Leap, Fenton!" cried the cousins.

So he lurched a[...]
out of reach of[...]
back of a very [...]

Gurgle glub, [...]
alligator's m[...]

"Jump, Fer[...]

So he heaved and he hurdled high in the air, narrowly escaping the alligator's snapping red jaws, and landed right in the middle of a family of haughty white egrets.

Slip slap, Slip slap, Flip flap, Flip flap went their snowy-white wings. And away Fenton leaped from the fanning wings, hoping he'd land on a soft lily pad.

And so he did, floating round and round and round until the sun set orange-red behind the whispering pine trees.

Dragonflies hummed by Fenton's small ears with a *whirr, whirr, whirr* and a *whing, whing, whing*.

Clouds of mosquitoes zigged and zagged with a *zee, zee, zee* and a *zing, zing, zing*.

And through the moist night air Fenton heard
the insults of the many swamp frogs:

"Clumsy, clumsy swamp frog,
  Knee deep, knee deep, knee deep
You never will be free.
  Knee deep, knee deep, knee deep
Clumsy, clumsy swamp frog,
  Knee deep, knee deep, knee deep
You cannot see to seeeeeeeeee."

Lurch, Splat, Blat, Drop, Plop went Fenton, until one day he went flopping into a fisherman's line, snapping it in half and setting free one very unhappy catfish.

And with that he turned, leaped and flopped smack into the trunk of a fat umbrella tree.

The grateful catfish blew a stream of bubbles in the murky water, and swam close to the bank where Fenton sat in the cool brown mud of the lush green swamp under the tree.

"Katy Catfish is my name.
Scavenging swamp bottoms
is my game."

And with a flashing twist and a silver turn, she went streaking through the black swamp waters leaving Fenton blinking blindly in the white bright sun. Far away the rumble of thunder sounded in the sky.

In less than two squawks of a marsh crow, Katy parted the waters in ripples and rolls and flipped from her mouth into the air a gleaming pair of gold-rimmed spectacles that had rested for years on the slimy swamp bottom.

Over and over they turned, glinting in the sun until they landed on the nose of Fenton, who still sat in the cool mud blearily blinking in the very hot sun.

Another rumble of thunder rippled through the swamp. Swamp grass trembled and black crows filled the air.

Fenton blinked once, then twice, as the sky darkened. A flash of lightning crackled through fast-gathering clouds.

Fenton looked at the cool greenness behind him. He looked at the dark waters in front of him. He looked at the cloud-swollen heavens above him and began to croak a frog song that drowned out the pealing thunder and could be heard all across the wide, wide swamp.

"The world is beautiful.
    Knee deep, knee deep, knee deep
And I am free.
    Knee deep, knee deep, knee deep
I can leap, I can soar, I can see,
    I can seeeeeeeeeeeeeeeeee!"

And for the first time Fenton really saw the yellow wildflowers and the white water lilies. He saw the umbrella trees and the pine trees and the soft green ferns.

He saw the egrets and the alligators and the dragonflies and the swamp crows and the little clouds of mosquitoes. He saw the streaks of lightning and then the raindrops dancing on the lily pads.

Splish, Splash, Splosh went the cousins and
Splish, Splash, Splosh sailed Fenton right behind them,
croaking his joyous song in the glistening rain, where he
touched every lily pad in a swamp that had turned pink
and gold under one very large rainbow.